D0194870

Summer Camp Queen

by Marci Peschke

illustrated by Tuesday Mourning

PICTURE WINDOW BOOKS
a capstone imprint

Kylie Jean is published by Picture Window Books
A Capstone Imprint
1710 Roe Crest Drive
North Mankato, Minnesota 56003
www.capstonepub.com

Library of Congress Cataloging-in-Publication Data
Peschke, M. (Marci)
  Summer camp queen / by Marci Peschke ; illustrated by Tuesday Mourning.
    p. cm. -- (Kylie Jean)
  Summary: School is over and Kylie Jean and her cousin Lucy are going to summer camp for a week of fun, but a girl named Miley seems determined to spoil the experience for everyone, and Kylie decides to discover what her problem is.   5209 5196 8/13
  ISBN 978-1-4048-7583-8 (library binding)   ISBN 978-1-4795-1531-8 (ebook)
  1. Camps--Juvenile fiction. 2. Children of divorced parents--Juvenile fiction. 3. Acting out (Psychology)--Juvenile fiction. 4. Friendship--Juvenile fiction. [1. Camps--Fiction. 2. Divorce--Fiction. 3. Behavior--Fiction. 4. Friendship--Fiction.] I. Mourning, Tuesday, ill. II. Title. III. Series: Peschke, M. (Marci) Kylie Jean.
  PZ7.P441245Sum 2013
  813.6--dc23   2012028533

Graphic Designer: *Kristi Carlson*
Editor: *Beth Brezenoff*
Production Specialist: *Eric Manske*

Design Element Credit:
Shutterstock/blue67design

Printed in the United States of America in North Mankato, Minnesota.
092012
006933CGS13

For Kenzie, with love for Rick
—MP

Table of Contents

All About Me, Kylie Jean!

My name is Kylie Jean Carter. I live in a
big, sunny, yellow house on Peachtree Lane in
Jacksonville, Texas with Momma, Daddy, and my
two brothers, T.J. and Ugly Brother.

T.J. is my older brother, and Ugly Brother
is . . . well . . . he's really a dog. Don't you go
telling him he is a dog. Okay? I mean it. He thinks
he is a real true person.

He is a black-and-white bulldog. His front looks
like his back, all smashed in. His face is all droopy
like he's sad, but he's not.

His two front teeth stick out, and his tongue hangs down. (Now you know why his name is Ugly Brother.)

Everyone I love to the moon and back lives in Jacksonville. Nanny, Pa, Granny, Pappy, my aunts, my uncles, and my cousins all live here. I'm extra lucky, because I can see all of them any time I want to!

My momma says I'm pretty. She says I have eyes as blue as the summer sky and a smile as sweet as an angel. (Momma says pretty is as pretty does. That means being nice to the old folks, taking care of little animals, and respecting my momma and daddy.)

But I'm pretty on the outside and on the inside. My hair is long, brown, and curly.

I wear it in a ponytail sometimes, but my absolute most favorite is when Momma pulls it back in a princess style on special days.

I just gave you a little hint about my big dream. Ever since I was a bitty baby I have wanted to be an honest-to-goodness beauty queen. I even know the wave. It's side to side, nice and slow, with a dazzling smile. I practice all the time, because everybody knows beauty queens need to have a perfect wave.

I'm Kylie Jean, and I'm going to be a beauty queen. Just you wait and see!

Chapter One

The Saddest Day Ever

Today is the last day of school before summer vacation. I can't believe that all of my fun school days are over for this year! While I finish getting dressed, I think about how much I am going to miss my teacher, Ms. Corazón, and my bus driver, Mr. Jim.

Momma hollers, "Kylie Jean, breakfast is ready!"

"Yes, ma'am," I call.

Ugly Brother barks, "Ruff, ruff." Two barks means yes.

I look at him, all wiggly and full of excitement. He's glad school is nearly over and we can play every single day of the summer. Summer days are longer than regular days. We can play until it gets dark outside, but I'm not sure I'm ready for summer just yet!

"You better be good until I get home," I tell him. "Then we can play tag in the backyard."

I head downstairs. In the kitchen, there are some pretty roses in butterfly paper on the counter. I press my nose into the bouquet, taking a deep breath.

I gasp. "Momma, these flowers smell like heaven!"

Momma laughs. "Well, I don't know about that, but I do know your teacher is an angel," she says. "Now, if you don't hurry and eat your breakfast, Mr. Jim will have to wait for you."

I eat three spoons of fruity rings cereal before I hear the bus pull up in front of my house and the horn goes BEEP, BEEP!

I grab my backpack and run for the door. Then I have to run back because I forgot my teacher's flowers. I can't forget those!

When we get to school I see my best cousin, Lucy. We walk to class together. She is feeling a little blue about the end of school, too.

It's hard to stay sad, though, because our teacher has a surprise for us! Lucy spots them first. She asks, "Do you see those bags on our desks?"

"Sure do!" I reply. We can't wait to see what's inside them, so we skip right over and look.

I peek in.

The first thing I see in my bag is a book. That makes me happy. I just know that beauty queens love to read. They like to read so they can be extra smart.

Lucy dumps her bag out on the table. Candy, a toy ring, bookmarks, and other goodies scatter over her desk like little birds in the sky.

"Yay!" Lucy shouts.

Cara and Paula run over. "We're having a pizza party, too!" Cara says.

Paula adds, "And cupcakes!"

We are so excited we can hardly wait.

The day zooms by. After lunch we get to play
board games. I like old-fashioned checkers. Pa
taught me how to play like an expert. I'm always
red and Lucy is always black.

While we play, I have a great idea! "Do you
know what I'm thinking?" I ask Lucy. "Wouldn't
pink checkers be just divine?"

Lucy says, "Well, the boys
wouldn't like them,
but I would."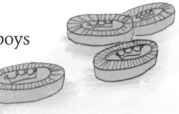

When the three o'clock bell rings, I can't believe
it. Just like that, school is over.

Lucy starts to cry a little. She does that
sometimes. Reaching over, I give her a squeezy
hug.

I whisper, "Don't be sad. Just think about all of the swimming you're going to do this summer."

Maybe I am trying to convince myself, too! I don't say much on the bus. Mr. Jim is probably worried about me, since I usually talk all the way home. He doesn't know that the last day of school is the saddest day ever!

At home, I drag my backpack into the kitchen.

"Don't be so down, darlin'," Momma says. "I think I have something to cheer you up."

Then she hands me an envelope. I tear it open.

Congratulations!

You have won a scholarship to the
Mariposa Ranch Girls' Summer Camp!

Campers will spend a fun-filled week
at Lake Mariposa.
We can't wait to meet you!

Our Motto:

Flitter, flutter, flee, you can't catch me!
I create, inspire, and achieve.
I'm a Mariposa girl!

I'm over the moon with happiness. Momma
went to Mariposa Ranch Camp when she was
a girl, and she tells me that Lucy is going to go
with me. My saddest day ever just turned into the
happiest day ever!

Chapter Two
Calling All Campers

One week later, I am packing for camp! They sent me a list of things to bring. I'm using my prettiest pink pencil to check off each thing that I put in my duffel bag. That way I won't forget a single important thing!

The first thing I pack is my sleeping bag. It's pink. Granny sewed my name on it and decorated it with a pretty little crown. Then I check my list.

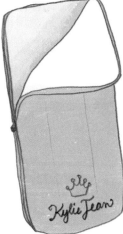

Things to Bring to Camp:

1. clothes
2. sneakers, flip-flops
3. towel
4. bathing suit
5. hair brush, shampoo
6. toothbrush, toothpaste, soap
7. flashlight, batteries
8. stamps, envelopes, pencils, pens, paper
9. water bottle
10. bug spray
11. sunblock
12. raincoat
13. backpack
14. laundry bag
15. magazines, books
16. sleeping bag, blanket, and pillow

Then I pack my clothes. Momma wrote my name inside all of my shirts and shorts with a black marker. They're easy to pack because I fold them first.

T.J. comes in with a flashlight. He says, "I just put batteries in this for you. Use it when you walk at night, so you don't step on a snake or anything."

I groan. "Are you tryin' to scare me, T.J. Carter?" I ask.

"Nope," he says. "I'm just warnin' you to be careful. That's all. Have fun, too!"

Going to camp seems like a huge adventure. My head is so full I can hardly go to sleep for wondering and wondering about this and that.

But before I know it, morning comes and I am all loaded up in the truck.

Momma and Daddy are both taking me to camp. I let Ugly Brother kiss me goodbye, because I am going to miss him so much. He looks lonely sitting in the driveway when we leave. I have to think about making new friends or I might  just start to cry like a baby, and I haven't even had to say goodbye to Momma or Daddy yet.

We drive and drive and drive some more, right into the pine woods.

"Look!" Momma says. She points out the window at a sign that says, "Welcome to Mariposa Ranch Camp." The letters are green and all around the edge are painted butterflies.

Daddy pulls into a parking spot. We climb out, unload, and tote all my stuff over to a tall girl with a clipboard.

"Hey, y'all," she says. "I'm Jane Ellen, camp counselor."

"Nice to meet you," I tell her. "I'm Kylie Jean, future queen."

She laughs. "I like your spunk, girl." Then she checks her list. "All the cabins are named after butterflies. You are in the American Lady Butterfly cabin. And aren't you lucky, I'll be your counselor! Follow that path and you'll see it at the end."

When we open the door to my cabin, I see a big room with eight beds. Then I get the best surprise ever. My cousin Lucy is an American Lady, too! We scream with happiness when we see each other. Now I won't be so sad when Momma and Daddy leave.

Momma gives me a hug. "Be sweet and have fun," she says. "And don't forget to write home. Okay?"

"Okay, Momma," I say. "I'll write home every day."

Daddy kisses the top of my head and says, "Bye, sugar bean. I love you to the moon and back."

"I love you a bushel and a peck!" I reply.

Quick as a wink, they hit the road for home. Then Lucy and I introduce ourselves to the other girls in our cabin. Their names are Ella, Pearl, Annabelle, Maggie Mae, Lola, and Charlotte.

Pearl asks, "Who's a first timer?"

Lucy and I both raise our hands. All of the other girls have been here before.

"You're going to just love camp," Ella says. "It's so much fun!"

Suddenly, we hear a bell ringing and ringing, just like Nanny and Pa's dinner bell.

Pearl says, "That bell means they're calling all campers. It's time for our welcome dinner."

"We better go or we'll be late and lose points," Charlotte says.

She explains that they have a contest at the camp to see who gets the most points. That girl gets to rule the camp for a day.

"Kylie Jean already has lots of experience being a queen," Lucy tells the other girls. "She'd be a great ruler!"

Ella says, "No one from this cabin ever won the contest before. Usually a Monarch wins."

"There's a first time for everything!" I say, but no one agrees with me.

Just then, Jane Ellen walks in. "You heard the bell, girls," she says. "Let's go!"

We head down the path to the dining hall. As we pass the Monarch cabin, I see a girl who looks just like me!

But that can't be true. It must be my imagination playing tricks on me.

Inside the dining hall, there are two lines for food trays. We American Ladies get in the line to the right. Just as we get to the end of our line with trays full of cook-out chow, I come face to face with myself!

The girl looks at me and I look at her. She lifts her tray and I lift mine. She blinks and I do, too. That's when I see that her eyes are brown, not blue like mine are. In every other way, she looks just like me! Momma always says everyone has a twin somewhere.

"Hi," she says. "I'm Miley."

I smile. "Hi," I say. "I'm Kylie Jean."

She says, "I bet you made that up. Your name can't really be Kylie. Don't ever bother me again, got it?"

She spins around and marches over to the Monarchs' table.

Lucy's mouth is hanging open so wide she could catch flies.

"What just happened?" she asks.

All I can do is shrug.

The rest of our first night at camp goes as smooth as the lake on a calm day. We play games and get to know each other.

Camp is going to be real fun!

Dear Momma and Daddy,

My cabin has six other really nice girls in it. Tonight we ate hot dogs and played games. It was fun! You'll never believe it, but there is a girl here who looks just like me, except she has brown eyes. Her name is Miley. Nanny would probably say she's a handful. Now that it is time for bed I wish I could come home, but tomorrow when I am having fun I know I'll be glad I'm at camp.

Love,

Kylie Jean

XOXOXOXO

P.S. Please give a hug and kiss to Ugly Brother for me.

Chapter Three
First Day Fun

The next morning, we're eating a huge breakfast of flapjacks, eggs, and bacon. I see my "twin" at the Monarchs' table.

She sticks her tongue out at me! I'm tempted to stick mine out, too, but then I remember I'm a lady, so I don't.

The camp leader stands up. Her name is Missy.

Miley is busy yawning. Her counselor, Amanda, tries to get her to pay attention, but she won't.

Missy says, "I want to welcome y'all to camp again and remind you that camp is what you make it. Play hard, try new things, and make life-long friends. Everyone should follow the camp rules at all times. Now, I know you can't wait to get out there. Today, campers, you can choose the ropes course or horseback riding. Before we dismiss you, Jane Ellen will explain our Ruler for the Day competition."

Jane Ellen explains that campers get points for every activity they complete. We can get extra points for good behavior. Also, points can be deducted for bad behavior or poor sportsmanship. The camper with the most points on the day of the Jamboree will get to rule the camp for one day.

Then we all say the camp motto. "Flitter, flutter, flee, you can't catch me. I create, inspire, and achieve. I'm a Mariposa girl!"

I grab Lucy, because an idea just hit my brain like a saddle on a horse! If I do both riding and the ropes course, I can get more points. The more points I have, the better my chances are of ruling the Mariposa Ranch.

"Let's do both activities!" I beg.

Lucy agrees. "Okay," she says, "but only because I know being a queen is your big dream."

One by one, each cabin gets dismissed by their counselor. When it's our turn, Jane Ellen says, "Get out there and have some first-day fun!"

Lucy has to chase me to the stables, because I run the whole way there.

We saddle up our horses ourselves. We're country girls, so we know how to saddle, ride, and groom a horse.

Caroline is the counselor at the stables. She says, "Wow! You did a great job. Five points each."

Then we ride all the way down to the lake and back. Miley must be at the ropes course, because we don't see her.

When we're done riding, we brush our horses down and get another five points. Now Lucy and I have ten points each.

It's time to go to the ropes course. Amanda is the counselor at the ropes course. Miley and the Monarchs have not made it through the course yet. It must be hard!

Amanda explains, "The ropes course has high and low parts. You need a partner to spot you for the high course. Are you two partners?"

Lucy and I say, "Yup!"

Amanda gives us a map of the course and we're ready to go. We do the low course first. There is a zigzag, which is really like walking on a beam, except it's not a straight line. We zip right through that part.

Then we put on blindfolds and go through a maze. First I give Lucy directions so she can get through it. Then she gives me directions.

Next is the whale watch. It looks like a giant teeter-totter, and together we have to try to balance it. The wall is straight ahead. It's a giant wooden mountain that we have to climb over. Lucy groans. "I'm tired," she says. "How are we ever going to climb over that wall?"

"Come on!" I say. "We're not quitters."

Three splinters and ten tries later, we still are not over the wall. Now I'm ready to quit, too.

Some other girls have shown up. One of them, Bailey, suggests, "Let's help each other."

"What's your plan?" I ask.

Bailey says, "Let's build a pyramid and let one girl climb up and over. Then she can help us from the other side."

"Count us in!" Lucy says.

Working as a team, we get every single girl over the wall.

The last challenge is climbing a rope with knots in it. We did this in gym class, so I know just what to do. You have to pull yourself up with one hand over the other. If you look down from the top, you might get scared!

When I'm done, Lucy takes her turn. But her arms aren't strong enough. Even with me cheering, she doesn't make it. "That's okay," she says. "I tried hard."

Amanda gives us each five points for trying, plus three points for teamwork. I get two points for finishing the whole course, but no one else does.

"Only one other girl has finished the whole thing," Amanda says.

"Who?" I ask.

You guessed it! Miley the Monarch.

I try not to worry about Miley. I have twenty points. That's pretty good for one day at camp!

Dear Ugly Brother,

I promised to write you a letter and here it is!
They do not have any dogs at camp, but they do have
butterflies, bees, mosquitoes, flies and every other kind
of bug. I know you would love to dog paddle in Lake
Mariposa.

Today we rode horses. Don't get jealous, though. Okay?

I missed you all day long. I bet you miss me, too.

We are having a contest and I have 20 points now.

Give Momma and Daddy a kiss for me. I love you all
more than cheese and grits!

Hugs and kisses, your sister,

Kylie Jean

Chapter Four
Cabin Chaos

The next day when Miley finds out I have twenty points, it starts a little war between the Ladies and the Monarchs. The other girls tell me that Miley is from Houston. That girl is a city slicker and I'm a country gal. No wonder we're so different. I try not to worry about it. We have a busy day making crafts.

Each cabin designs a t-shirt. The American Ladies paint one big butterfly with white stars on the wings.

Everyone gets to vote on their favorite shirt.

Miley shouts, "Vote for the Monarchs! Our shirt rules!"

"Vote for the Ladies!" I holler. "Be true blue!"

The Ladies chant, "Ladies, LADIES, LADIES!"

Belle sighs, "I just love craft day. It's the most fun!"

One of the counselors counts the votes. We don't win. The winners each get five points. That makes me start to worry that I might lose my lead in the contest!

The next project we make is friendship bracelets.

When no one else is looking, I see Miley dump the box of thread onto the floor. It looks like she just spilled a rainbow.

Luckily, her counselor notices, too. She says, "Miley, you just lost five points."

Miley shrugs like she doesn't care. I don't understand that girl. She acts like she wants points, but then she does something she knows will get her into trouble.

Lucy notices, too. She asks, "Why did she do that?"

"I was just asking myself that same question," I say. "It's a mystery. Maybe we can figure it out."

Lucy and I help pick up all the thread, because pretty is as pretty does.

We were raised up to be helpers and have good manners. Our good deed earns us each one point, but we didn't do it for the points!

Then we make our bracelets. They're easy to do. You just braid the thread just like you would your hair. I make mine pink, all pink. Some of the thread is a soft baby pink, some is hot pink like watermelon, and I add bright bubblegum pink too. When I'm done, I make bracelets for each of the Ladies.

Counselor Caroline exclaims, "What a nice thing to do for your cabin sisters! I'm going to give you a point for each one. Eight points."

"Yay!" I say. "Thank you."

Lucy gives me a high five. She knows I'm in the lead. But she's not the only one who knows that.

That night, when we're all getting ready for bed, Maggie slides into her sleeping bag and hops right back out like a jackrabbit, screaming.

She points to her feet. They are covered with shaving cream. That is a city girl trick if I ever saw one!

Lola frowns. "I bet that Miley girl is behind this," she says. "She doesn't like us. Do you think she's trying to get kicked out of camp?"

"We can't let them get away with this, or we'll be in for a really long week," Pearl says.

Belle thinks for a minute.

Then she says, "You know, I believe I just saw a grass snake on my way back from the showers."

The girls and I look at each other.

"What do you think those city girls will do with a snake?" Lola asks.

"I bet they'll scream, run, and cry," Lucy says, "and in that order, too."

"Let's get it," Lola says. She and Belle creep out of the cabin.

Sure enough, minutes later we hear some screams and then some crying, too.

Soon, the counselors are in our cabin. No one admits to putting the snake in the cabin. Even the girls in Miley's cabin say that it must have just slithered in.

Part of me feels bad, though. I shouldn't have let them put that snake in the other girls' cabin.

Each cabin gets inspected. I'm sure we'll pass just fine, but then Jane Ellen goes through my bag. "There's a whole sack of junk food in here," she says.

I'm shocked, and so are the rest of the girls.

"Looks like Miley got the last laugh this time," Pearl mutters.

I lose three points, but the worst part is that the other girls in my cabin do, too.

I feel terrible.

Jane Ellen looks disappointed. "I'm surprised that you would be a rule breaker," she says to me.

I want to tell her that I'm not a rule breaker, but I don't want to argue.

"Tomorrow is a new day and you can start fresh," Jane Ellen says. "Try to be a better camper."

Dear Miss Clarabelle,

I am writing to you by flashlight. The girls in my cabin all just went to sleep, even Lucy. We are in the American Lady cabin. You are the finest lady I know, so I sure wish you could help me out.

There is a girl here who looks just like me with brown eyes. Her name is Miley and I'm sad to say that when I'm around her I act like a brat. But the worst part is how awful she acts to me. I've been getting into trouble and it isn't even my fault.

I am wondering what in the world to do about it.

If you were here, you would probably say two wrongs don't make a right.

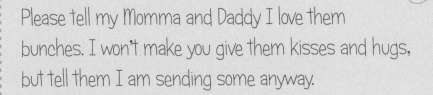

Please tell my Momma and Daddy I love them bunches. I won't make you give them kisses and hugs, but tell them I am sending some anyway.

Your friend and neighbor,

Kylie Jean

Chapter Five
Campfire Sing-a-long

In the morning I start out by being on my very best camp behavior. I don't want to get into trouble. That means I have to try real hard to not even look at Miley.

Lucy notices. She asks, "Are you trying not to let Miley get you into any more trouble?"

I reply, "Yup!"

"That's a great plan," she says. "How can I help?"

I shrug. "I just want to stay out of trouble all day," I tell her. "Avoiding Miley seems like a good beginning."

The first thing we do after breakfast is design flags for our cabins. We have a head start since our cabin is practically named after the good ol' U. S. of A.

The flag is easy to make. We draw our faces instead of the stars. There isn't enough room for fifty stars anyway.

In the afternoon we write campfire songs. Tonight is a big camp sing-along.

At first, we don't know how to start. Then Ella starts to scribble on her paper.

We all wait . . . and wait . . . and then she sings.

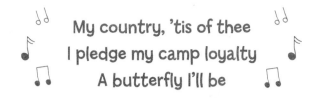

My country, 'tis of thee
I pledge my camp loyalty
A butterfly I'll be

My sisters we will sail and watch for our mail
We'll make some crafts and play
Look at nature on another day

And when it's time to go
We'll miss each other so
Loyal ladies we will be
We'll make camp history!

Belle gasps. "That's amazing!" she says.

I nod. "Wow!" I say. "You can do all the writing for our cabin. You're awesome."

Ella blushes. "Thanks, y'all," she says. "I do want to be a writer when I grow up."

"You already are!" Lucy says.

After we write a few more songs, we help find sticks to roast weenies and marshmallows on. Lucy and I skirt around the edge of the camp, looking for sticks in the woods. The leafy trees are like green umbrellas shading us from the sun. We walk and we chat.

Luckily, we're not so busy talking that we can't pay attention. Miley is walking near us, and she starts reaching for a stick that's in a bunch of poison ivy!

"Not that one!" I yell. "Poison ivy alert!"

She still reaches for it. I hold my breath.

"Why should I believe you?" Miley asks.

Lucy rolls her eyes. "Think about it," she tells Miley. "If Kylie Jean wanted to make trouble for you, she'd keep quiet and let you be all covered with an itchy red rash. She's trying to help you out!"

Slowly, Miley backs away from the stick. She says, "Fine! I'll look somewhere else."

We watch her go the other way and I'm glad. My plan is to stay away from trouble. As far away as I can get! "Trouble should be that girl's middle name," I say.

Lucy nods and says, "I think you're right!"

Later that night, much later, when the long summer day ends and the sky is a dusky gray dusted with glitter of soon-to-be stars, we head over to the fire pit for our campfire.

The counselors have piled up the wood in the center like a little teepee and the top of it blazes red, orange, and yellow fire. I spot Jane Ellen sitting next to our American Ladies flag. On the other side of the fire are Miley and the other Monarchs. I feel relieved that we're not side by side.

It's time for s'mores! I roast my marshmallows until they are charred black on the outside and melted inside. When I stack them up with a chocolate bar and graham crackers, they taste like heaven.

Then an idea hits my brain like a hungry skeeter on a camper. "Let's tell ghost stories!" I suggest.

All around the fire, campers shout out, "Yes!"

"Kylie Jean is a good storyteller," Lucy says. "Let her go first!"

I stand up in the eerie glow of the firelight. The shadows dance around us like monsters. Then I begin with a voice as soft as a whisper, so everyone has to lean in to hear me. Everyone loves my creepy tale.

Caroline suggests a storytelling contest, so a few more campers tell stories.

Lucy whispers, "None of them can hold a candle to yours, Kylie Jean."

After a few more creepy stories, the camp leader, Missy, stands up. She says, "I am giving ten points to the best storyteller. Let's vote. The camper with the most clapping and cheering when I call her name will be the winner."

When she calls my name, it gets so loud I bet they can hear us as far away as Dallas.

Missy smiles and says, "Ten points to Kylie Jean!"

Hurray! I am well on my way to being queen of Mariposa Ranch!

Dear T.J.,

Tonight I won a campfire storytelling contest.
You sure gave me some good ideas. Remember all the
times you tried to scare me? Well, I used all of the best
ideas in my story for the contest tonight.

I sure do miss everyone. especially Momma and Daddy
and Ugly Brother. Tell Momma and Daddy that I will
write them a letter tomorrow.

I love them more than s'mores!

Your sweet little sister,

Kylie Jean

XOXO

Chapter Six
Game Day

In the morning, we hear the gentle tapping of rain on the tin roof of our cabin when we wake up. Maggie Mae sits up and arches her back like a cat stretching. Sleepily, she asks, "Is it raining?"

BOOM! Thunder shakes our cabin walls!

"I don't think we'll be having a water sports day today," Belle says. She looks disappointed.

"If we can't go to the lake, what can we do?" Lucy asks.

Pearl explains, "They'll have a game day inside, since the weather is bad outside."

After breakfast, we find out that Pearl is right. We are going to have a game day. There are games stacked on the tables, like Monopoly, Chess, Checkers, Sorry, Candy Land, and Life.

We Ladies stick together. First we play Sorry. It's a fun game and not too hard to play. Miley loses the game at her table, so she knocks all the game pieces onto the floor!

Jane Ellen crosses her arms and frowns. "Miley, that wasn't very good sportsmanship," she says. "You need to learn that everyone is a winner, but only one girl can win the game!"

Miley shrugs and mutters, "Whatever."

Lola whispers to me, "She has a bad attitude!"

Next we play Monopoly. It takes a lot longer. You would not believe how rich Pearl gets. She likes to buy things, so she buys a lot of property, houses, and hotels. Almost any space you land on belongs to Pearl.

When someone lands on a space, we chant, "Pay Pearl!"

"Look at all your money!" I say. "Looks like you're the Queen of Cash! I bet you're going to be the winner."

Pearl nods. "I bet I do win," she says. "My family plays this game all the time. Every time we play, I'm the winner!"

Even though we all know that Pearl is going to win, we keep playing. It's fun just hanging out together.

Pearl does win, of course. Then Lucy and I move on to Tic-Tac-Toe. Lucy and I start a game first. Then all of the other American Ladies decide to play, too. I am the X and Lucy is the O. We keep score. At first I am in the lead with seven wins, but then Lucy starts to catch up.

After a few games, we decide to have a Tic-Tac-Toe Tournament. Soon all of the girls from the other cabins are playing Tic-Tac-Toe, too! The girls who win the most will play against each other.

By the end of game day we are all awarded ten points each. Well . . . almost all of us. Since she was a bad loser earlier, Miley only gets five points.

I'm starting to feel sorry for Miley. She has a hard time controlling her feelings!

Dear Momma and Daddy,

I miss you so much!

It rained today. Nanny would say it rained cats and dogs. We played games inside all day. I won the Tic-Tac-Toe tournament.

I saw more of my look-alike twin. We might look the same on the outside, but we are not at all alike on the inside. I think that girl has a bee in her bonnet. I am trying to be extra good.

I love you to the moon and back!

Your little queen,

Kylie Jean

P.S. Read this letter to Ugly Brother and give him a kiss from me.

Chapter Seven

Splish Splash

In the morning, the pale yellow sun floats low over Mariposa Lake. No rain! Today will be a great day for water activities.

After breakfast we all go back to our cabins to change into our swimsuits. We're going to have swimming relays, go canoeing, and have a picnic.

Lucy and I are kind of nervous, since we've never been in a canoe before. We've only been in Pa's little motorboat, fishing on the big lake.

There is a narrow path that leads down to the water. One by one we head down the path. From above we probably look like ants on a log!

When we get to the beach, I start to feel less nervous about the canoes. There's a lot to do in the water. Campers can swim a relay out to the raft and back. There are huge, black inner tubes for floating lazily along and a tire swing for daredevil girls who want to swing out over the lake and jump off into the cool blue water.

The Ladies start with the swim relay. We are racing against the Monarchs. Lucy starts the relay. Then it's Pearl's turn.

While Lola goes, we dog paddle in the shallow water.

We all chant, "Lola! Lola!"

I'm last and so is Miley. Lola tags me first and I'm off!

We have to swim using three different strokes. I start with the butterfly stroke, move on to the forward crawl, and finish with the backstroke. It seems like Miley is copying me until the end, when she does a side stroke.

The backstroke lets me use my legs for extra speed at the end, but Miley edges ahead by a hair and the Monarchs win. They each get ten points.

The Ladies are disappointed, but we give the other team high fives and congratulate them anyway. We aren't poor losers!

Next we head over to the canoes. Each canoe has a name on its side.

Lucy and I want the pink one named Butterfly Breeze. But some other girls get to it before we do, so we decide to wait until they get back. While we wait, we grab inner tubes and float along, watching our friends race their canoes.

Lucy and I hold hands so we won't float apart. I drag my free hand in the water. We float along watching until the Ladies win! YAY!

By then our pink canoe is back, but it's lunchtime, so we head for the shore. The cook has made a picnic lunch for us to eat right beside the lake. Each cabin has a picnic basket.

Ella says, "I wonder what's inside!"

Wrapping my towel around my waist, I say, "I hope it has watermelon in it."

"I want brownies!" Pearl shouts.

Charlotte looks inside and starts pulling things out of the basket.

Lucy says, "Looks like we have ham and cheese sandwiches, carrot sticks, watermelon, and chocolate chip cookies."

Right away we start to stuff ourselves with picnic food.

"I'm so hungry I could eat a whale after swimming in that race!" I say.

Lucy laughs. "A whale could eat you," she says, "but you couldn't eat a whale."

For a while there is more eating than talking as we munch our lunch. When we are finally done, we clean up our mess.

Then we head over to the canoes. Luckily, Butterfly Breeze is waiting for us.

Lucy and I learn the hard way that unlike motorboats, canoes are tippy. She gets in first and gives me her hand. As I pull it, the canoe tips toward me, and Lucy falls out!

Splish splash! Her head pops up out of the water.

"That was scary!" she shouts.

I nod. "Let's both try to get in at the same time," I suggest.

"Okay," Lucy agrees.

That way, everything goes as smooth as lemon cream pie! Then we paddle around the lake after a few quick paddling lessons. If we paddle together, we can go fast enough to make ripples in the water that look like little waves.

On our little canoe trip, we see birds on the shore, fish in the water, and a little island.

We paddle back to shore. Then we walk the narrow trail back to our cabin. We are tired from our busy day in the water.

Dear Ugly Brother,

Today was water sports day! You would have loved it. I know how much you like to dog paddle. You know what? I learned how to paddle a canoe today. It's not as easy as it looks.

You would have a hard time, because canoes wobble a lot. Also, it is hard to get in and out of them without falling into the water. Lucy fell in today! Don't worry, though. Okay? She is just fine.

I miss you to the moon and back times a zillion.

Love and doggie treats,

Kylie Jean

Chapter Eight
Double Trouble

The next day is nature day. After breakfast, all of the campers head over to the edge of the woods. Our camp leader, Missy, is in charge.

"I'm going to love nature day," I say.

"How do you know?" Belle asks.

I shrug. "I'm a country girl," I tell her, "and country girls love being outside in nature!"

Lucy giggles. "Me too, then!" she says.

Missy calls each cabin and gives us our first activity. The American Ladies will be doing the nature walk first. "And tomorrow," she says, "is our camp jamboree. We will award our Spirit Stick to the cabin that's shown the most spirit here at Mariposa Ranch."

Missy waves the Spirit Stick in the air. It is a sparkly silver tube filled with little bells that make noise when you move it. On the end of the stick are ribbons with little beads on the ends. We American Ladies want that Spirit Stick bad!

We walk over to the start of the nature trail. Counselor Amanda gives us a backpack with a first aid kit, map, and whistle. She says, "If you follow the trail you should be back in an hour and ready to move on to tree planting."

Charlotte suggests, "Let's pair up with a buddy."

Right away Lucy and I pair up. Then we're off!

The dirt path is marked with little wooden arrows pointing the way. Even though the day is warm the woods are cool under the green, lacy trees. Ella knows a lot about nature. She points out the different plants and trees along the way. There are a LOT of pine trees in the woods.

We stay on the path and try not to get lost. Sometimes I stop to pick up a pretty little rock, a leaf, or smell a flower.

There are some flowers with delicate little petals. I wonder what kind they are. They're so pretty and sweet.

Before we know it we are back where we started.

Amanda says, "You made it in forty-five minutes. That's a record! Great job!" We all cheer. Amanda adds, "You've earned five points."

Next, we head to the tree-planting spot. Tree planting is dirty work. First we have to dig a hole. I am good at digging. Sometimes I help Ugly Brother when he needs to bury something.

We wedge the shovel into the sandy dirt and scoop it away. It takes a long time to dig a hole that's big enough to plant a tree in. Then we knock the extra dirt off our tree's roots.

I bet you can guess what kind of tree it is. A pine tree!

When we're done, that's another five points, and it's time for lunch.

After lunch, it's time for nature crafts. We can choose the craft we want to do. Our choices are leaf stamp cards, picture frames with pecan shells glued on them, and wall hangings made of twigs and string.

I can't decide. I ask Lucy, "What are you going to do?"

Lucy replies, "I think a frame would be nice. Then I could put my camp picture in it."

"I think I'll make cards," I say. "I've been sendin' letters home, and a card would be nice instead."

I choose lots of different colors of green paint to make my leaf prints with. The leaves are all lovely shapes. Some are long and narrow. Some are fat and round. The prints will look just like the leaves do in nature. They'll remind me of summer camp.

When all my cards are finished, I leave them to dry and go wash my hands. Now I have fifteen points for the day.

Our last stop is bird watching. That's something you do by yourself, alone. Otherwise you are tempted to chat and scare the birds off.

Counselor Caroline gives me a sketch pad and binoculars. "Find five birds, sketch them, and try to name them," she tells me.

I choose a path that's a little overgrown and head down it.

First, I see a tiny hummingbird no bigger than a blossom near a buttercup. Its wings flutter so fast it looks like it is floating in the air.

When I walk a little farther, I hear a woodpecker tapping on a dead tree. Walking and watching has drawn me deep into the woods.

Then I gasp. Right before me is a tiny shimmering waterfall that trickles into a stream tucked between moss-covered rocks.

The sun shines like a lantern, straight through a gap in the canopy of the trees.

Beside me is a stump surrounded by little pink flowers.

This is a peaceful, magical spot. The waterfall babbles happily. I sigh. Right now I wish I could build a little cottage and live here forever.

In the distance, I hear a mockingbird. They can sing out like almost any other bird. While I'm sketching the mockingbird, I see a little brown wren. She will be my last bird sighting for today.

When I am finished, I wander back to camp.

I feel happy. I liked my bird-watching walk. But everyone looks worried when I walk out of the woods. Lucy runs over to me. She sputters out, "They think you stole it! The Spirit Stick. One of the counselors saw you do it."

I am shocked. At first, all my words are stuck in my mouth.

"I know you wouldn't do that," Lucy says. "Right?"

I look across the clearing and see Miley. She's wearing tan shorts and a green Camp Mariposa t-shirt, just like I am.

Missy comes over looking mad as a hornet. She asks, "Kylie Jean, did you steal the Spirit Stick? Tell me the truth."

I shake my head. "No ma'am!" I say, looking up at her. "It wasn't me. I was bird watchin' in the woods."

Missy frowns. She asks, "Was Lucy with you?"

"No, ma'am," I say quietly. "I went alone."

Missy wants to look in my cabin. That's fine by me since I know I'm not hiding a Spirit Stick.

The other American Ladies and I wait outside the cabin. They know I'd never do something so terrible.

"It's going to be fine," Ella says.

Pearl nods. "That Spirit Stick isn't in our cabin, so when Missy doesn't find it, she'll know you didn't take it," she says.

Then we hear bells.

Missy comes out of the cabin, holding the Sprit Stick. "This was under your pillow," she says. "Kylie Jean, I'm taking away all of your points."

A tear slips from my eye. "I didn't take it, ma'am," I say. "I really didn't."

"Stealing is wrong," Missy says. "I hope you will think twice before taking something that is not yours in the future!"

The tears sting my eyes as Missy walks away. Lucy pats my back. "Now I won't get to be queen," I say. "And everyone thinks I'm a thief."

"No way," Lucy says. "We're not going to let this happen, are we, girls?"

"No way," the other girls say.

But I'm not so sure. I think this really might be the worst summer ever.

Dear Momma,

A terrible, awful thing happened today. I wish you could come and take me home. Miley, my look-alike, did something bad and everyone thinks it was me.

I lost all my points, but the worst part is that people won't trust me unless I can prove that I didn't do it.

I'm as sad as an owl without a tree. Tomorrow I have to find a way to get Miley to tell the truth.

Maybe when I write my next letter everything will be worked out. I hope you believe I'd never do something so terrible.

Love,

Kylie Jean

Chapter Nine
Jamboree

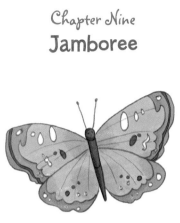

The next morning, I wake up before everyone else. Then I slip quietly down to the lake. Sitting on the dock, I tuck my legs under me. I need to do some powerful thinking.

Suddenly, I hear something behind me. It's Miley!

"What are you doing out here?" she asks.

I shrug. "Thinkin' about what to do next," I say.

She sits down beside me and plays with the laces on her shoes. Neither one of us says anything for a while, but soon I can't take it anymore.

"Miley, why did you put that stick under my pillow?" I ask.

She is quiet at first, but then she starts to talk and talk and talk.

She tells me that her parents aren't married anymore and it makes her feel like a ping-pong ball. She goes to her mom's house, then she goes to her dad's apartment, and after that she does it again.

Her mom and dad don't even notice her, because they are too worried thinking about themselves. The only time they say anything to her is when she gets in trouble.

"That explains why you like trouble so much," I say.

"I thought I could get sent home if I lost too many points," she admits. "But they just keep giving me another chance."

I nod my head, but one thing has me puzzled. I ask, "Why did you make it look like I stole the Spirit Stick when YOU wanted to get in trouble?"

Miley lets out a big sigh. "At first, I thought if I stole the stick they'd send me home for sure," she says. "But then, after I took it, I got nervous. I got so nervous I decided I better get rid of it. I was going to hide it in the woods. Then one of the counselors saw me with the spirit stick. I had to think of something fast."

"You thought of me!" I say.

Miley nods.

"You decided that if you put it in my cabin they would think I did it," I go on. "We had on the same outfit yesterday and no one was close enough to see your brown eyes."

She nods again and whispers, "That's right."

I look right at Miley. "I know you like trouble," I tell her, "but I don't. The only way to fix this is for you to tell the truth."

She gasps and says, "Confess?"

"It's only fair," I say. "You're the one who did it. And two wrongs don't make a right. That's what my momma always says."

"That's what my momma says, too," Miley says. "Or at least she used to."

She lets out a big sigh and shrugs. "I guess if they send me home that's what I wanted anyway," she says. "I guess my momma and daddy will notice that."

That gives me an idea.

I ask, "Have you ever tried to be so good that your parents notice you?"

Miley frowns. "No," she says. "I don't think it would work."

"You should try it," I say. "Besides, it makes you feel good inside when you do good things, even if no one on the outside cares."

I reach over and give Miley a little hug. "I guess what I'm tryin' to say," I tell her, "is that you can notice yourself."

"I never thought about it like that," Miley says. She stands up to leave. "Thanks, Kylie Jean."

"Are you going to tell them you did it?" I ask.

She shrugs and gives me a little wink. "Maybe I will," she says, "and maybe I won't."

At breakfast, Missy tells us campers she has a special announcement. I cross my fingers and hold my breath.

"Someone has admitted to taking the Spirit Stick and putting it in another cabin," Missy says.

I look at Miley. She smiles a little. Then I give her a thumbs up. Even though Missy doesn't say who did it, everyone knows. If it wasn't me, it had to be my look-alike twin.

"Kylie Jean," Missy says, "you can have your points back."

Yay! I still have a chance to rule the camp for a day. That means I might get to be a camp queen after all.

That evening at the camp jamboree, we make foil packet suppers to cook on the hot coals of the fire. I put potatoes, carrots, and chicken in mine.

While the packets cook, we have entertainment. Some of the counselors play the guitar and we sing songs. The other American Ladies and I put our arms around each other's shoulders while we sing.

Then we eat our steaming packets of food. Eating outside makes food taste delicious!

Once we clean up the supper mess, each cabin takes a turn on the stage. We are going to sing the song that Ella wrote, but we're going last.

The first girls do a cheerleading routine. They jump, toss, and flip around on stage. Wow! We cheer and clap extra loud!

Next, Miley's cabin does a skit. They say it's called "Butterfly Girl and the Three Counselors." It's like Goldilocks and the Three Bears, but they change it to a camp story. It is very clever.

Did you guess that Miley is the Butterfly Girl? It is the perfect role for her since she used to love trouble so much.

When they're done, we whistle and shout extra loud.

The next cabin tells a ghost story. Lucy thinks it is almost as good as mine was. We yell and stomp extra loud.

When it's our turn, we pass out papers with the words to our song. Then we sing it out loud and proud. Everyone loves it. Even the counselors and Missy sing along.

At the end of our Jamboree Celebration, Missy goes onstage to make the announcement I've been waiting for. She says, "The cabin with the most spirit is the American Ladies!"

We scream, jump up, and run to the stage. Charlotte is a speedy runner, so she gets there first. We pass the Spirit Stick around and each Lady gives it a shake. The bells rattle and ring.

Then Missy says, "This year's contest winner and camp ruler for the day is Kylie Jean Carter! Tomorrow, she'll rule Camp Mariposa!"

Everyone cheers.

I give the campers my best beauty queen wave,
nice and slow, side to side. I'm so happy to be a
queen!

Dear Family,

My look-alike told the truth! I'm not in trouble
anymore, and y'all will be so proud of me. Tonight at the
jamboree, all my hard work paid off. I won the contest!

That means I am camp ruler tomorrow.

In my next letter, I will tell you all about it. I am a little
sad that tomorrow is our last day at camp, but I'm
going to try not to think about it for now.

Love you bunches,

Kylie Jean - Camp Queen

Chapter Ten
Queen for a Day

The next morning, I get up early. I'm so excited I hardly slept a wink!

I dress in my favorite pink t-shirt and pull my tiara out of my bag. It's been waiting there all week, just in case I needed it.

I like to take it everywhere. Good thing! I can't be a queen without it!

The first thing I do is ask the cook to make her famous cinnamon sugar donuts for all the other girls.

When everyone arrives for breakfast, I greet them at the door to the dining hall with my best beauty queen wave.

After everyone sits down, I get to make a little speech. Lucy gives me a thumbs up. Jane Ellen winks at me as I go to the front of the room.

"The first thing I want to do as ruler is let y'all know I prefer to be called Camp Queen, your highness, or her majesty," I say. I look around. Everyone looks nervous. I can tell they think I'm going to be the bossiest queen ever.

"I have wanted to be a queen since I was an itty bitty baby," I go on.

Lucy claps for me, and I smile at her.

"The next thing I wanted to tell you is very important," I say. All the girls and counselors are looking at me now. I take a deep breath and say, "I'm going to make each of you a queen, too! We can rule this camp together!"

Everyone cheers. They are so excited!

"My orders for the day are to make this the best day at camp," I say. "Don't forget to include your counselor."

I sit down with the American Ladies. "What should we do today?" I ask.

Maggie Mae says, "How about swimming, your majesty?"

"I love that idea, your highness!" I reply.

Then we all get the giggles. The day might get a little confusing with so much royalty around.

"It is very exciting to be queen," Lola says. "Now I know why you like it so much."

Pearl nods. "Being a queen makes me feel so special," she says.

"Let's go to the lake and have a picnic," Lucy suggests. "We could have brownies this time."

Charlotte wants to take another canoe trip, and Belle wants a bonfire.

Our day is going to be fantastic!

Ella asks, "Are you going to wear your crown in the water, too?"

"Yup!" I reply.

The Ladies laugh when I get in an inner tube wearing my pink striped bathing suit and a tiara. "A well-dressed queen always has a tiara," I explain, "but because I'm wearin' it, I won't go swimmin', just floatin'."

Next we have our picnic on the shore. We shake out a red checked cloth and sit around the edges with our food in the middle.

Then we enjoy fried chicken legs and potato salad, plus rich chocolatey brownies for dessert. Pearl wants to eat all of the brownies by herself, but we convince her to share them.

When we have eaten everything but the crumbs, Charlotte reminds us that we need to find our favorite pink canoe. Then we paddle happily around the lake singing camp songs.

We're tired when we're done with our canoe trip, but we still have time for a bonfire before bed. We gather sticks, and then Jane Ellen piles the sticks together and sets a blaze.

We watch the sun set like a tangerine against a watermelon sky. Lucy gets out the marshmallows, graham crackers, and chocolate bars for the s'mores.

I jab three sticky white puffs on my stick and listen while we each share what we've loved most about Mariposa Ranch Camp.

As the night creeps in around us, we get quiet for the first time all day and I see tiny flashes of light like a million little blinking stars.

I whisper, "Look, fireflies!"

In the quiet darkness, we are filled with marshmallows and happiness.

Dear Momma and Daddy,

Today was the best day of summer camp.
We were all queens all day! Our day was filled with
fun. Each girl picked out something she wanted to do.
At first I was afraid we might not have enough time
to do everything, but just like magic, we did it all.

I have been creative, done a lot of things, and been a
leader for a day. I think I'll always be a Mariposa girl.

I can't wait to see you tomorrow and tell you more!

Love,

Kylie Jean

Marci Bales Peschke was born in Indiana, grew up in Florida, and now lives in Texas with her husband, two children, and a feisty black-and-white cat named Phoebe. She loves reading and watching movies.

When **Tuesday Mourning** was a little girl, she knew she wanted to be an artist when she grew up. Now, she is an illustrator who lives in South Pasadena, California. She especially loves illustrating books for kids and teenagers. When she isn't illustrating, Tuesday loves spending time with her husband, who is an actor, and their two sons.

Glossary

achieve (uh-CHEEV)—do something successfully

binoculars (buh-NOK-yuh-lurz)—an instrument that you look through to make distant things seem nearer

convince (kuhn-VINSS)—make someone believe you

counselor (KOUN-suh-lur)—someone trained to help campers

course (KORSS)—a series of events or tasks

decorated (DEK-uh-rate-id)—added something to make an object look prettier

divine (duh-VINE)—wonderful

eerie (IHR-ee)—strange and frightening

experience (ek-SPIHR-ee-uhnss)—something that happens to you

inspire (in-SPIRE)—to encourage and influence someone

scholarship (SKOL-ur-ship)—a prize that pays for something

sportsmanship (SPORTS-muhn-ship)—fair and reasonable behavior while playing a sport

Talk!

1. Kylie Jean had a hard time getting along with Miley. What could she have done to make this better?

2. Have you gone to summer camp? If not, do you want to? Talk about your experiences with camp.

3. What do you think happens after this story ends? Talk about it!

Be Creative!

1. Kylie Jean's dream is to be a beauty queen. What's your number-one dream?

2. Who is your favorite character in this story? Draw a picture of that person. Then write a list of five things you know about him or her.

3. In this book, Kylie Jean writes lots of letters. Choose a favorite person to write a letter to.

This is the perfect treat for any summertime queen!
Just make sure to ask a grown-up for help.

Love, Kylie Jean

From Momma's Kitchen

PERFECT SUMMMERTIME LEMONADE

YOU NEED:

1 cup sugar

1 cup water

1 cup lemon juice (fresh or from a bottle)

3 1/2 cups cold water

ice cubes

a grown-up helper

1. In a small saucepan, mix 1 cup water and 1 cup sugar. Ask your grown-up helper to cook, stirring occasionally, until the sugar has dissolved. Let this simple syrup cool.

2. In a pitcher, mix the syrup and the lemon juice. Add the cold water until it's the perfect taste (you might need a little more or a little less).

3. Serve over ice cubes in tall glasses.

Yum, yum!

Kylie Jean

has one BIG dream . . .
to be a beauty queen!

Available from Picture Window Books
www.capstonepub.com

THE FUN DOESN'T STOP HERE!

Discover more at www.capstonekids.com

- ♥ Videos & Contests
- ❀ Games & Puzzles
- ♥ Friends & Favorites
- ❀ Authors & Illustrators

Find cool websites and more books like this one at www.facthound.com. Just type in the Book ID: **9781404875838** and you're ready to go!